Dr. Seuss's real name was Theodor Geisel.
On books he wrote to be illustrated by others,
he used the name Theo. LeSieg,
which is Geisel spelled backward.

www.randomhouse.com/seussville

Library of Congress Cataloging-in-Publication Data
LeSieg, Theo., 1904–1991.
The eye book / by Dr. Seuss, writing as Theo. LeSieg ; illustrated by Joe Mathieu.
    p.   cm. — (A bright and early book)
SUMMARY: A boy and rabbit both have two eyes that see all kinds of things,
from blue and red to a bird and a bed.
ISBN 0-375-80033-6 (trade). — ISBN 0-375-90033-0 (lib. bdg.)
[1. Vision—Fiction. 2. Eye—Fiction. 3. Rabbits—Fiction. 4. Stories in rhyme.]
I. Mathieu, Joseph, ill. II. Title. III. Series: Bright & early book.
PZ8.3.L54934Ey 1999 [E]—dc21 98-25120

Printed in the United States of America   21

BRIGHT & EARLY BOOKS, RANDOM HOUSE, and the Random House colophon are
registered trademarks of Random House, Inc.

The EYE BOOK

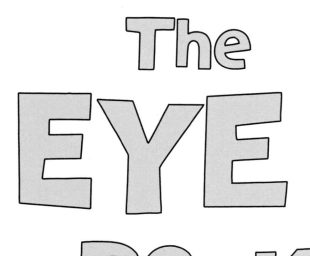

By Dr. Seuss*
*writing as
Theo. LeSieg

Illustrated by Joe Mathieu

A Bright and Early Book
From BEGINNER BOOKS
A Division of Random House, Inc.

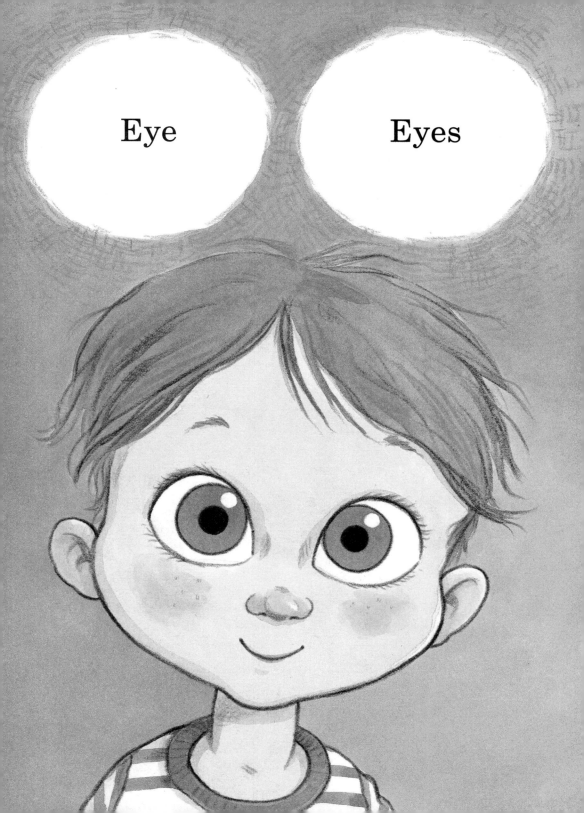

My eyes
My eyes

His eyes
His eyes

Wink eye
Wink eye

Pink eyePink eye

My eyes see.

His eyes see.

I see him.

And he sees me.

Our eyes see blue.

Our eyes see red.

They see a bird.

They see a bed.

They see the sun.

They see the moon.

They see a fork

a knife

a spoon.

They see a girl.

They see a man...

a boy

a horse

an old tin can.

They look down holes.

They look up poles.

Our eyes see trees.

They look at clocks.

They look at bees.

They look at socks.

Our eyes see flies.

Our eyes see ants.

Sometimes they see
pink underpants.

Our eyes see rings.

Our eyes see strings.

They see
so many, many things!

So many things!

Like rain

and pie...

and dogs

and airplanes
in the sky!

And so we say,
"Hooray for eyes!
Hooray, hooray, hooray…

...for eyes!"

DR. SEUSS (who was known as Theodor Geisel when he wasn't writing or drawing) wrote and illustrated 44 books for children and their lucky parents. But sometimes Dr. Seuss liked to write books and have someone else draw the pictures. For those books he used the pen name Theo. LeSieg (which is